In the beginning there was no fire
on Earth, and the world was cold.

The Sky People had fire.
But they lived high up in
the mountains, and guarded
it from the animals.

"Who will steal the fire?"
asked the animals, when
the leaves began to fall
and the cold winds blew.

HOW RABBIT STOLE THE FIRE

RETOLD AND ILLUSTRATED BY

JOANNA TROUGHTON

This story of Rabbit and how he brought fire to the earth comes from the South East of the USA and is told by the Creek, the Hitchiti and the Koasati Indians. Stories of Rabbit the trickster and wonder worker are found in all the areas of the Mississippi from Hudson Bay to the Gulf of Mexico.

The bison was strong.
The wolf was cunning.
The bear was brave.
The wildcat was fierce.

But Rabbit was leader
of them all in mischief.

Rabbit made himself a wonderful
head-dress. Each feather, every
stitch he coated with pine resin.

"Here I go," said Rabbit, putting
on the wonderful head-dress.
And off he went to the village
of the Sky People. As he went
he sang a song. "Oh, I am going
to fetch the fire, to fetch the
fire, to fetch the fire." For that
is what he was going to do.

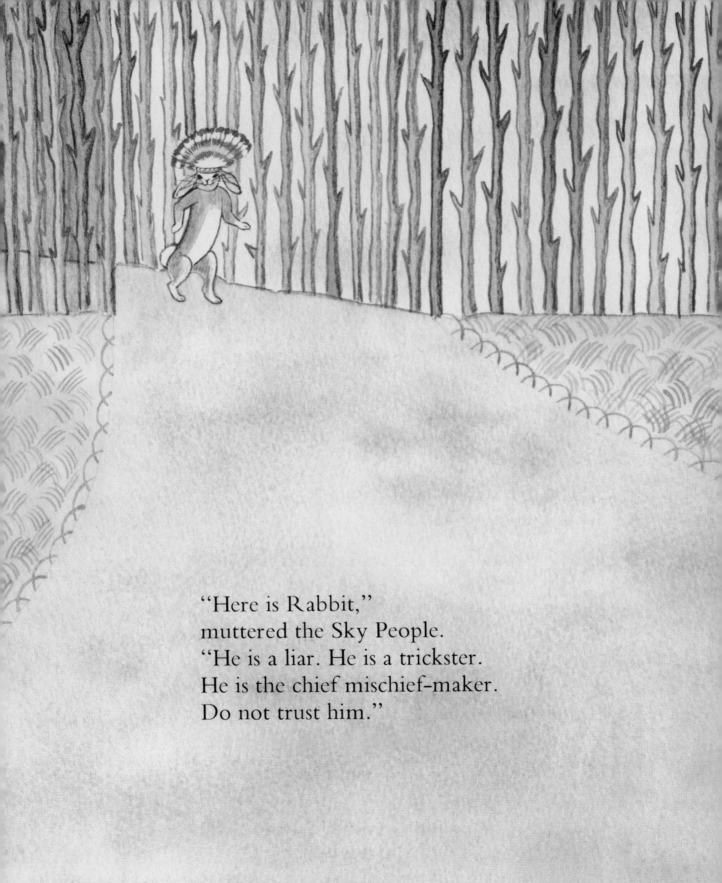

"Here is Rabbit,"
muttered the Sky People.
"He is a liar. He is a trickster.
He is the chief mischief-maker.
Do not trust him."

"Hallo, Sky People," said Rabbit.
"I have come to teach you a new dance.
Look at my dancing hat.

It is a dance to bring the corn from
the earth. It is a dance to guide
the fish to your nets."

So spoke Rabbit the trickster.
And with his words he soothed the Sky
People. He charmed them. He flattered them.

They forgot that he was a mischief-maker
and welcomed him into their village.
"Rabbit shall lead us in the dance!"

So Rabbit led the dance!
Round and round the fire
danced Rabbit. And round and
round behind him danced the
Sky People. Round and round
danced Rabbit, wearing his
wonderful head-dress . . .

and as he danced, he bent low
to the fire, singing his
dancing song. And the Sky
People bent low also.
Round and round danced Rabbit,
and very low he bent . . .

Whoosh! The head-dress was alight!
And away raced Rabbit, out of
the village and down the mountain.
"We have been tricked!" screamed the
Sky People. "Rabbit has stolen the fire!"

Rabbit ran and the Sky People followed.

They made a great rain.

They made thunder
and lightning.

They made sleet.

They made snow.

But the wonderful head-dress with the
resin-coated feathers burned brightly.

Rabbit was soon tired.
"Squirrel! Take the head-dress,"
he gasped. Squirrel took
the head-dress and ran.

As she went, the heat made
her tail curl up and over her back.
And so are squirrels to this day.

Squirrel was soon tired.
"Crow! Take the head-dress,"
she chattered. Crow took the
head-dress and flew. As he
went, the smoke turned
all his feathers black.
And so are crows to this day.

Crow was soon tired.
"Racoon! Take the head-dress,"
he cawed. Racoon took the head-dress
and ran. As she went, some ash
burned rings around her tail and face.
And so are racoons to this day.

Racoon was soon tired.
"Turkey! Take the head-dress,"
she panted. Turkey took the head-dress
and ran. As he went, the fire
burned all the feathers off his head
and neck. And so are turkeys to this day.

But Turkey was not a fast runner,
and the fire began to die.

"Set my tail alight," said Deer.
For in those days deer had long tails.

Deer took the fire on her tail,
and ran so fast that she made a wind
to fan the flames. Deer cried
to the trees as she passed,
flicking her tail this way and that,

"Trees, hide the fire!"
The trees took the fire and
hid it in their wood. But the
fire had burned off most of Deer's
tail. And so are deer to this day.

The Sky People returned to their
village high in the mountains.
Wood had hidden fire and they
didn't know how to find it again.
But Rabbit, leader of all mischief,
knew. It was he who showed the
animals how to find fire again
by rubbing two sticks together.
Now the animals have fire to
warm the cold winters, and light
to brighten the dark nights.